Team Spirit

# THE CLEVELAND BROWNS

BY

MARK STEWART

Content Consultant
Jason Aikens
Collections Curator
The Professional Football Hall of Fame

NORWOOD HOUSE PRESS

CHICAGO, ILLINOIS

Norwood House Press
P.O. Box 316598
Chicago, Illinois 60631

For information regarding Norwood House Press, please visit our website at:
www.norwoodhousepress.com or call 866-565-2900.

All photos courtesy of AP Images—AP/Wide World Photos, Inc. except the following:
Exhibit Supply Company (7 & 18); Topps, Inc. (9, 19 top, 22, 29, 34, 35 top, 36, 40 top & 43 );
Bowman Gum Company (14, 20 & 37 bottom); Author's collection (19 bottom & 40 bottom);
TCMA, Inc. (21); Photofest (31).
Special thanks to Topps, Inc.

Editor: Mike Kennedy
Designer: Ron Jaffe
Project Management: Black Book Partners, LLC.
Special Thanks to Jamie Feldman

LIBRARY OF CONGRESS CATALOGING-IN-PUBLICATION DATA

Stewart, Mark, 1960-
  The Cleveland Browns / by Mark Stewart ; with content consultant Jason
Aikens.
     p. cm. -- (Team spirit)
  Summary: "Presents the history, accomplishments and key personalities of
the Cleveland Browns football team. Includes timelines, quotes, maps,
glossary and websites"--Provided by publisher.
  Includes bibliographical references and index.
  ISBN-13: 978-1-59953-064-2 (library edition : alk. paper)
  ISBN-10: 1-59953-064-3 (library edition : alk. paper)
  1.  Cleveland Browns (Football team : 1946-1995)--History--Juvenile
literature.  I. Aikens, Jason. II. Title. III. Series: Stewart, Mark, 1960-
Team spirit.
  GV956.C6S74 2007
  796.332'640977132--dc22
                                      2006015332

Manufactured in the United States of America.

**COVER PHOTO:** Antonio Bryant celebrates a touchdown catch with teammate
Jeff Faine during a 2005 game against the Chicago Bears.

# Table of Contents

SPORTS WORDS & VOCABULARY WORDS: In this book, you will find many words that are new to you. You may also see familiar words used in new ways. The glossary on page 46 gives the meanings of football words, as well as "everyday" words that have special football meanings. These words appear in **bold type** throughout the book. The glossary on page 47 gives the meanings of vocabulary words that are not related to football. They appear in ***bold italic type*** throughout the book.

# Meet the Browns

The Cleveland Browns are one of the oldest teams in the **National Football League (NFL)**. They are also one of the newest! This is because, after 50 seasons in Cleveland, the Browns left the city and became the Baltimore Ravens. A new team called the Cleveland Browns joined the NFL in 1999. They share their history with the old Browns, and have won over a whole new generation of fans.

The Browns play in the **North Division** of the **American Football Conference (AFC)**. It is a rugged division, with very good defensive teams, including two **Super Bowl** winners, the Baltimore Ravens and Pittsburgh Steelers. When winter arrives, each game is a battle for survival.

This book tells the story of the Browns—both old and new. Every time they take the field, they become a part of one of the greatest *traditions* in football. Win or lose, every player gives everything he has, because the city and its fans expect nothing less.

Kirk Chambers, Braylon Edwards, and Corey McIntyre
celebrate after a Cleveland touchdown.

# Way Back When

In December of 1945, sports fans in the city of Cleveland were celebrating their first **NFL Championship**. Their joy soon turned to sadness when they heard that their champion Rams had decided to leave Ohio and move to Los Angeles, California. With so many fans hungry for football, it did not take long for another team to move into Cleveland—the Browns.

The Browns were part of the new **All-America Football Conference (AAFC)**. They were coached by Paul Brown, a young man who understood how the game was changing. He knew that **pro football** would get faster and more complicated. There would be more passing, and many different types of defenses. So respected was Brown that the team was actually named after him!

Brown went out and found a group of players whose skills would be perfect for the new game. Several of these players were African-Americans, a group that had been *barred* from the NFL since the 1930s. Led by quarterback Otto Graham, running back Marion Motley, and kicker Lou Groza, the Browns became the best team

Marion Motley

in the AAFC. They won the championship each year from 1946 to 1949, and lost only four games during those seasons.

After the 1949 season, the Browns, San Francisco 49ers, and Baltimore Colts were invited to join the NFL. The Browns won their conference each year from 1950 through 1955, and again in 1957. They won the NFL Championship three times during this period.

The Browns had great talent during the 1950s. Besides Graham, Motley, and Groza, the team featured many **All-Pro** players, including Bill Willis, Frank Gatski, Don Colo, Len Ford, Don Paul, Dante Lavelli, Horace Gillom, Ray Renfro, Mac Speedie, and Dub Jones.

A new era began when the Browns drafted running back Jim Brown. He played from 1957 to 1965, and led the NFL in **rushing** every year but one. In 1964, Brown teamed with **receivers** Paul Warfield and Gary Collins, and quarterback Frank Ryan, to win another NFL Championship.

Over the next 30 years, the Browns put many more good players on the field, including Leroy Kelly, Jerry Sherk, Don Cockroft, Brian Sipe, Greg Pruitt, Joe DeLamielleure, Ozzie Newsome, Matt Bahr, Bernie Kosar, and Michael Dean Perry. However, the team was unable to win the league championship again.

In 1995, team owner Art Modell stunned fans when he announced plans to move the Browns to Baltimore, Maryland, where they would eventually become the Ravens. The NFL promised Cleveland a new team that would carry on its tradition and history.

**ABOVE**: Jerry Sherk, the team's best defensive player during the 1970s.
**LEFT**: Jim Brown runs the ball during a game against the New York Giants.

# The Team Today

In 1999, Cleveland fans got the team they were promised. The "new" Browns were an **expansion team**. They were allowed to take some extra players from other NFL clubs, then added **college draft picks** and **free agents**. Their first coach was Chris Palmer. Their first stars were quarterback Tim Couch, receiver Kevin Johnson, linebacker Jamir Miller, and defensive linemen Ebenezer Ekuban and Courtney Brown.

Although the Browns were playing in a new stadium, it still came alive each Sunday with the same old energy and excitement. Cleveland's *love affair* with its football team picked up right where it had left off.

In only their fourth season, the Browns made it to the **playoffs**. It was a wonderful reward to the fans of Cleveland, who had waited patiently for their new team to arrive—and who had rooted for the Browns through good times and bad.

The Browns are now busy building a new football tradition. To do this, they are keeping one eye on the future and one eye on the past. Their goal is to recapture the spirit of Cleveland's glory years.

Charlie Frye and Dennis Northcutt enjoy a victory on their home field in 2005.

# Home Turf

The team has played in Cleveland Browns Stadium since 1999. The grass field is a blend of four types of grasses, which were scientifically tested to work in the city's **climate**. Cleveland gets very cold in the winter and very humid in the summer. A heating system under the field keeps the turf from freezing during the winter.

The seats behind the east end zone of Browns Stadium are reserved for a group of fans that call themselves the "Dawg Pound." During the 1980s, **defensive backs** Hanford Dixon and Frank Minnifield began calling themselves "Big Dawg and Little Dawg." Fans in one section started showing up to games dressed as dogs to show their support, and soon everyone started calling it the "Dawg Pound."

## BROWNS STADIUM BY THE NUMBERS

- *There are 73,300 seats in Browns Stadium.*
- *The Browns' locker room is one of the largest in the NFL at 11,000 square feet. The visiting team's locker room is 5,600 square feet.*
- *There are 147 luxury boxes in Browns Stadium.*
- *Browns Stadium was the first in the NFL to use a sand-and-soil base under its grass playing surface.*

Browns Stadium is located in the heart of downtown Cleveland.

# Dressed for Success

The Cleveland Browns have used the same team colors since they began playing in 1946—orange, white, and of course, brown. They wear orange helmets with a stripe running down the middle. In some years white helmets were used. In other years, player numbers were added to the sides of the helmets. Cleveland's uniforms have always featured stripes on the sleeves and pants.

The Browns were named after coach Paul Brown. However, their *logo* while he was with the team was a "brownie" holding a football and wearing a crown. A brownie is a tiny elf-like creature. The Cleveland brownie has never appeared on the team's helmet. In fact, the Browns are the only team today that has never used a helmet logo.

The Cleveland brownie was "retired" after Art Modell bought the team in 1962. He fired Coach Brown and got rid of the elf, too. Even so, the brownie continued to pop up here and there as the team's mascot. In 2005, the brownie returned to Cleveland. He began appearing on team gear and souvenirs, and fans were glad to have him back.

Frank Gatski and the Cleveland brownie share the front of this 1950s trading card.

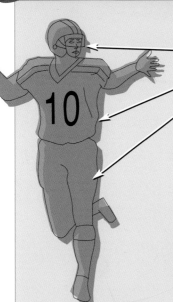

The football uniform has three important parts—

- Helmet
- Jersey
- Pants

Helmets used to be made out of leather, and they did not have facemasks—ouch! Today, helmets are made of super-strong plastic. The uniform top, or jersey, is made of thick fabric. It fits snugly around a player so that tacklers cannot grab it and pull him down. The pants come down just over the knees.

There is a lot more to a football uniform than what you see on the outside. Air can be pumped inside the helmet to give it a snug, padded fit. The jersey covers shoulder pads, and sometimes a rib-protector called a "flak jacket." The pants include pads that protect the hips, thighs, *tailbone*, and knees.

Football teams have two sets of uniforms— one dark and one light. This makes it easier to tell two teams apart on the field.

Braylon Edwards slips out of a tackle. The pads of a receiver are smaller than those of other players. This helps him move faster.

# We Won!

No football team has ever started as well as the Cleveland Browns did. They won their first seven games in 1946 and finished the year with a 12–2 record. In the **AAFC Championship**, Otto Graham passed the Browns to a 14–9 lead over the New York Yankees late in the game, and then intercepted a pass on defense to kill New York's final **drive**. One year later, the same teams met for the AAFC title, and the Browns won again, 14–3.

In 1948, the Browns won all of their 14 regular-season games—including three **road games** in eight days during November! They played the Buffalo Bills for the championship and destroyed them 49–7. Marion Motley was unstoppable in this game. He ran for 133 yards and scored three touchdowns. The team's perfect 15–0 record would not be equalled for 24 years. The Browns won their fourth and final AAFC crown in 1949 when they beat the San Francisco 49ers 21–7 in the championship game.

In 1950, the Browns became part of the NFL. Those who thought the AAFC was a weak league *predicted* that the team would struggle against "real" pros. The Browns proved them wrong. Cleveland finished 10–2, and then defeated the New York Giants

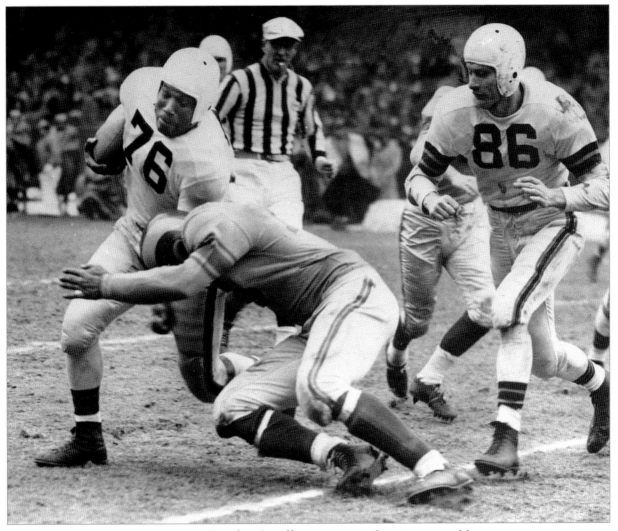

Marion Motley fends off a Los Angeles Rams tackler.

and Los Angeles Rams in the playoffs to become NFL champions. The Rams actually led the title game by one point late in the fourth quarter, but Lou Groza kicked a **field goal** with 28 seconds left to win the game 30–28.

Otto Graham

MADE IN U.S.A.

The Browns played for the NFL Championship again each year from 1951 to 1955. They lost to the Rams in 1951 and the Detroit Lions in 1952 and 1953, but in 1954 Cleveland defeated Detroit 56–10. Graham, who announced that this would be his last game, scored three touchdowns.

Coach Brown begged Graham to come back in 1955, and he agreed to play one more year. The team finished 9–2–1 to win its division for the tenth time in ten seasons. In the NFL Championship, the Browns played the Rams. The Cleveland defense chased Los Angeles quarterback Norm Van Brocklin all over the field, and Graham played a *magnificent* game to win 38–14.

The Browns rebuilt their team around running back Jim Brown in the late 1950s and early 1960s, and Blanton Collier replaced Paul Brown as head coach in 1963. In 1964, Cleveland reached the NFL Championship once again. The experts believed that they would

LEFT: Otto Graham, quarterback of the great Browns teams of the 1940s and 1950s. RIGHT: Gary Collins, the star of the 1964 NFL Championship. BELOW: A button that mistakenly shows the Browns as AFC Champs. They lost in the final seconds to Denver two years in a row.

lose to Johnny Unitas and the Baltimore Colts. The Browns played great defense and Gary Collins caught three touchdown passes from Frank Ryan in an amazing 27–0 victory.

GARY COLLINS

86

BROWNS

WIDE RECEIVER • A.F.C.

The Browns played for the NFL Championship again a year later, but lost to the Green Bay Packers. They played the Minnesota Vikings for the 1969 NFL Championship, but lost again. In 1970, the Browns, Colts, and Pittsburgh Steelers joined the American Football Conference (AFC). The Browns had excellent teams in 1986 and 1987. Cleveland fans thought their team was headed for the Super Bowl, but they lost the AFC Championship in both seasons to the Denver Broncos, who beat the Browns in the final seconds of each game.

# Go-To Guys

To be a true star in the NFL, you need more than fast feet and a big body. You have to be a "go-to guy"—someone the coach wants on the field at the end of a big game. Browns fans have had a lot to cheer about over the years, including these great stars…

## THE PIONEERS

### OTTO GRAHAM                                         Quarterback

- BORN: 12/6/1921    • DIED: 12/17/2003
- PLAYED FOR TEAM: 1946 TO 1955

A quarterback's job is to find a way to win, and Otto Graham did this better than anyone in the early years of pro football. He was a great passer and a powerful runner—and he also played defense for the Browns. Graham was the **Most Valuable Player (MVP)** twice in the AAFC and twice again in the NFL.

### MARION MOTLEY                                      Running Back

- BORN: 6/5/1920    • DIED: 6/27/1999    • PLAYED FOR TEAM: 1946 TO 1953

Marion Motley was one of the first "big backs." He was a fast runner and a great **blocker**. When Otto Graham dropped back to pass, Motley made sure no one laid a hand on him.

## LOU GROZA
### Kicker/Lineman

- BORN: 1/25/1924  • DIED: 11/29/2000
- PLAYED FOR TEAM: 1946 TO 1959 & 1961 TO 1967

Lou Groza was such a good kicker that he was nicknamed "The Toe." He also played the line for Cleveland for 14 years and was one of the league's best **tackles**. Groza was at his best when kicking to win a game.

## BILL WILLIS
### Lineman

- BORN: 10/5/1921  • PLAYED FOR TEAM: 1946 TO 1953

Bill Willis was the man who made the Browns' defense work. He played in the center of the team's **five-man line**, and was so quick and powerful that other teams did not dare run plays up the middle.

## JIM BROWN
### Running Back

- BORN: 2/17/1936
- PLAYED FOR TEAM: 1957 TO 1965

Jim Brown did one thing, and he did it better than anyone in history—he ran with the football. He was bigger than most NFL linebackers and had the speed of an Olympic runner. It usually took two or three tacklers to bring Brown down. He averaged more than five yards gained every time he touched the ball.

**LEFT**: Otto Graham  **RIGHT**: Jim Brown

## BRIAN SIPE                          Quarterback

• BORN: 8/8/1949    • PLAYED FOR TEAM: 1974 TO 1983

Brian Sipe was a great passer and respected leader. He battled through injuries to become one of the best quarterbacks in the NFL. Sipe led the league in touchdowns in 1979 and was the MVP in 1980.

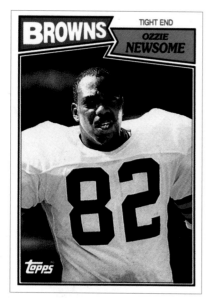

## OZZIE NEWSOME                     Tight End

• BORN: 3/16/1956

• PLAYED FOR TEAM: 1978 TO 1990

Ozzie Newsome was too big to be a wide receiver, so the Browns made him a **tight end**. He was a good blocker and a great pass-catcher. Newsome once caught at least one pass in 150 games in a row.

## MICHAEL DEAN PERRY              Defensive Lineman

• BORN: 8/27/1965    • PLAYED FOR TEAM: 1988 TO 1994

Michael Dean Perry was not as well known as his brother, William "The Refrigerator" Perry, but he was a very good player. He was a fierce tackler who made opponents worry on every play.

**ABOVE**: Ozzie Newsome   **TOP RIGHT**: Bernie Kosar
**BOTTOM RIGHT**: Willie McGinest

## BERNIE KOSAR                    Quarterback

- BORN: 11/25/1963
- PLAYED FOR TEAM: 1985 TO 1993

Bernie Kosar did not look like a star NFL quarterback. He was neither big nor fast, and he threw the ball with a strange slingshot motion. All he did was win—he never let up until the final whistle sounded. After Kosar retired, he helped bring a new team to Cleveland.

## WILLIE MCGINEST                 Defensive End

- BORN: 12/11/1971
- FIRST SEASON WITH TEAM: 2006

Willie McGinest helped the New England Patriots win three Super Bowls before he joined the Browns for the 2006 season. He was known for "shutting down" his side of the field and providing great leadership to his team.

# On the Sidelines

The Browns have had many of the NFL's top coaches over the years, including Blanton Collier, Forrest Gregg, Sam Rutigliano, Marty Schottenheimer, Bill Belichick, and Romeo Crennel. However, their first coach—Paul Brown—was their best. Brown was the most famous high school coach in Ohio during the 1930s, and proved himself during the 1940s at Ohio State University. He also coached a powerful team made up of soldiers at the Great Lakes Naval Training Station during World War II.

When Brown came to professional football, he brought some funny ideas with him. He believed in having a lot of **assistant coaches**, and he liked to give them a lot of responsibility. Brown liked to call plays from the sidelines instead of letting his quarterback decide what to do. He coached the team from 1946 to 1962.

Although Brown himself was a strict man with strict rules, he thought a good team should always be *flexible*. He designed plays for the offense that gave his players many *options*. And he designed a defense that could change its look to confuse opponents. These are just a few of the ideas Brown brought to pro football more than 50 years ago—and they are all important parts of the pro game today.

Paul Brown gets a victory ride from his team after the 1950 NFL Championship.

# One Great Day

The Browns were one of only three AAFC teams that survived a merger with the NFL in 1950. Many thought that Cleveland would only be a so-so team in the bigger, stronger league. Browns fans knew better. They could not wait for opening day, when the Philadelphia Eagles came to town. The Eagles were the NFL champions. If the Browns did well against them, they would earn the respect of all NFL fans.

The Eagles scored first when Cliff Patton kicked a field goal. The Browns took the lead when Otto Graham threw a long pass to Dub Jones, who scored a 59-yard touchdown. Cleveland scored again when Dante Lavelli cut between two defenders to catch a 26-yard touchdown pass from Graham. Another touchdown pass, to Mac Speedie, made the score 21–3.

The Browns had proved that they could pass against Philadelphia's great defense. For the rest of the game, they showed they could run the ball, too. Graham scored Cleveland's fourth touchdown himself, and Jones scored the final touchdown on a 57-yard run. The final score was 35–10. The Browns no longer had to prove themselves to anyone.

Otto Graham, who led his team to five touchdowns against the Eagles.

# Legend Has It

## Who made the greatest tackle in Browns history?

**LEGEND HAS IT** that it was Bill Willis. In the fourth quarter of Cleveland's 1950 playoff game against the New York Giants, running back Gene "Choo-Choo" Roberts broke through the Browns' defense and was running for the winning touchdown. Willis, a lineman, sprinted for more than 40 yards and dragged the shocked Roberts to the ground just before he reached the goal line. The Browns won the game 8–3, and then won the NFL Championship a week later.

# Who was the lightest NFL player of the last 25 years?

**LEGEND HAS IT** that it was Gerald McNeil of the Browns. McNeil stood 5' 7" and weighed just 140 pounds. He was the team's punt returner from 1986 to 1989, and one year he led the NFL with 49 punt returns. The biggest player of the 1980s was William Perry of the Chicago Bears, who weighed almost 350 pounds. Everyone called him the "Refrigerator." McNeil's nickname was—what else?—the "Ice Cube."

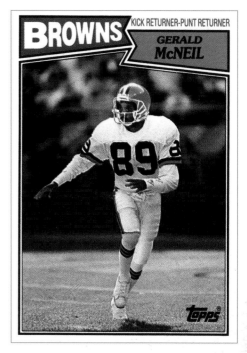

# Why are NFL reserve players said to be on a team's "taxi squad?"

**LEGEND HAS IT** that they actually drove taxis in Cleveland. The Browns' first owner, Art McBride, owned several taxi companies in the city. When a player was cut, McBride gave him a job driving one of his taxis. When the Browns needed a player to fill in, he simply rejoined the team.

**LEFT**: Bill Willis  **ABOVE**: Gerald McNeil

# It Really Happened

In the summer of 1966, Jim Brown was on top of the football world. He had been named the NFL's best player twice, and led the Browns to the NFL Championship in 1964. In 1965, Brown was the league's top runner, with 1,544 yards. It was the eighth time in nine seasons he had led the NFL in rushing.

However, Brown's mind was on something other than football that summer. He was a cast member of a movie called *The Dirty Dozen*, and was thinking about becoming a professional actor after he retired from the NFL. The question was, when was the right time to leave football?

Filming of *The Dirty Dozen* was delayed several weeks by rainy weather in England. Brown was supposed to **report** to training camp that July, but soon it became clear that he would be late. The Browns demanded that their star choose between his acting career and his football career.

Brown shocked the sports world when he announced that he had chosen acting. No one could believe that he would leave the NFL

Jim Brown (left) with movie stars Charles Bronson and George Kennedy.
This picture was taken during filming of *The Dirty Dozen*.

when he was still the league's best player. For Brown, the decision
was easy. Why wait for injury or old age to end your career when
you could go out on top? And be in a hit movie, too!

# Team Spirit

The football fans of Cleveland are among the most loyal in history. They rooted for the Rams from 1937 to 1945, until they moved to Los Angeles. They rooted for the old Browns from 1946 to 1995, until they moved to Baltimore and became the Ravens. When the new Browns came to Cleveland in 1999, more than 70,000 fans bought tickets to watch them play their first **preseason game**.

There are many football traditions in Cleveland. Fans are proud of their team, and have made the team colors part of their wardrobes. You can hardly walk down one of the city's streets without seeing someone dressed in orange and brown.

During games, many fans paint themselves in the team colors. Many more show their support by dressing like dogs and sitting in the team's famous "Dawg Pound." When a Browns player scores a touchdown, he sometimes jumps into the stands to soak up the love of the Cleveland fans.

Receiver Quincy Morgan celebrates his touchdown with Cleveland fans.

# Timeline

In this timeline, each Super Bowl is listed under the year it was played. Remember that the Super Bowl is held early in the year, and is actually part of the previous season. For example, Super Bowl XL was played on February 4 of 2006, but it was the championship of the 2005 NFL season.

**1948**
The Browns go undefeated and win their third of four AAFC titles.

**1954**
Otto Graham scores three touchdowns in the NFL Championship vs. the Detroit Lions.

**1946**
The Browns win their first game, against the Miami Seahawks, 41–0.

**1950**
Lou Groza kicks the winning field goal in the NFL Championship vs. the Los Angeles Rams.

**1957**
Jim Brown is voted the NFL's **Rookie of Year** and Most Valuable Player.

**1964**
The Browns win their fourth NFL championship vs. the Baltimore Colts.

The great Cleveland Browns team of the 1950s.

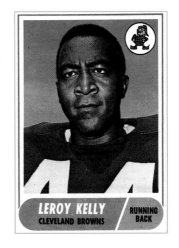

Leroy Kelly

**1968**
Leroy Kelly leads the NFL in rushing for the second year in a row.

**1988**
The Browns reach the AFC championship game for the second year in a row.

**1999**
The Browns rejoin the NFL as an expansion team.

**1979**
Quarterback Brian Sipe leads the NFL with 28 touchdown passes.

**1995**
The "old" Browns play their final season in Cleveland before moving to Baltimore.

**2002**
The "new" Browns make the playoffs in their fourth season.

Brian Sipe

Kenard Lang and Robert Griffith watch the clock tick down during the victory that sent them to the playoffs in 2002.

# Fun Facts

## NAME GAME

The Browns were originally going to be called the Panthers until someone remembered that a team with the same name had failed in Cleveland after just five games in 1926. A contest was held to rename the team, and the fans chose Browns in honor of their head coach, Paul Brown.

FRANK RYAN
CLEVELAND BROWNS    QUARTER-BACK

## BRAINIAC

Frank Ryan, the quarterback of the 1964 champions, might have been the smartest man ever to play in the NFL. He majored in **physics** in college and earned a **Ph.D.** in mathematics.

## BARRIER BREAKERS

In 1946, four African-American players broke pro football's "color barrier." Two—Bill Willis and Marion Motley—played for Cleveland. Paul Brown had coached both players in the past, and asked them to try out for the team. For the team's first game, in Miami, Brown benched Willis and Motley, fearing a **racial incident**.

## WHAT MIGHT HAVE BEEN

In 1962, the Browns drafted running back Ernie Davis, winner of the Heisman Trophy as the best college player. The thought of Davis and Jim Brown lining up together terrified Cleveland's opponents. Sadly, Davis was *diagnosed* with *leukemia* and died before he played a game for the Browns.

## FANTASTIC FINISHES

In 1980, 13 of the Browns' 16 games were decided by a touchdown or less—many in the final seconds. They were nicknamed the "Kardiac Kids" because of their heart-pounding finishes.

## STICKY STUFF

Dante Lavelli caught 386 passes for the Browns in the 1940s and 1950s, and almost never dropped a ball. His teammates nick-named him "Gluefingers."

**LEFT**: Frank Ryan  **TOP**: Ernie Davis  **RIGHT**: Dante Lavelli

# Talking Football

"As we came out and up the dugout steps, those 80,000 fans would roar. I mean *roar*. They shook that old stadium. I feel very lucky to have heard those kind of cheers. Few people do."

—*Paul Warfield, on the Cleveland fans*

"The test of a quarterback is where his team finishes."

—*Paul Brown, on what made Otto Graham great*

"There is no telling how much yardage I might have made if I ran as much as some backs do now."

—*Marion Motley, on how he would do in today's game*

**ABOVE**: Paul Warfield    **RIGHT**: Lou Groza

"The great thing was that we had men on our line who'd block once, then get up and keep blocking. I knew if I got past the line of scrimmage, those linemen were out there somewhere, blocking downfield. That gave me even more *incentive*."

—*Jim Brown, on how he led the NFL in rushing yards eight times*

"Never worry about missing a field goal. Just blame the holder and think about kicking the next one!"

—*Lou Groza, on how to deal with a poor kick*

# For the Record

T he great Browns teams and players have left their marks on the record books. These are the "best of the best"…

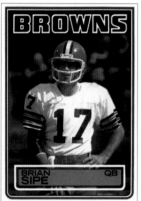

Brian Sipe

Paul Brown

## BROWNS AWARD WINNERS

| WINNER | AWARD | YEAR |
| --- | --- | --- |
| Otto Graham | AAFC Most Valuable Player | 1947 |
| Otto Graham | AAFC Most Valuable Player | 1948 |
| Paul Brown | AAFC Coach of the Year | 1949 |
| Otto Graham | NFL Most Valuable Player | 1951 |
| Paul Brown | NFL Coach of the Year | 1951 |
| Otto Graham | NFL Most Valuable Player | 1953 |
| Paul Brown | NFL Coach of the Year | 1953 |
| Lou Groza | NFL Most Valuable Player | 1954 |
| Otto Graham | NFL Most Valuable Player | 1955 |
| Jim Brown | NFL Rookie of the Year | 1957* |
| Jim Brown | NFL Most Valuable Player | 1957 |
| Paul Brown | NFL Coach of the Year | 1957 |
| Jim Brown | NFL Player of the Year | 1965 |
| Jerry Sherk | AFC Defensive Player of the Year | 1976 |
| Forrest Gregg | NFL Coach of the Year | 1976 |
| Sam Rutigliano | AFC Coach of the Year | 1979 |
| Brian Sipe | NFL Most Valuable Player | 1980 |
| Sam Rutigliano | AFC Coach of the Year | 1980 |
| Marty Schottenheimer | AFC Coach of the Year | 1986 |
| Michael Dean Perry | AFC Defensive Player of the Year | 1989 |

# BROWNS ACHIEVEMENTS

| ACHIEVEMENT | YEAR |
|---|---|
| Western Conference Champions | 1946 |
| AAFC Champions | 1946 |
| Western Conference Champions | 1947 |
| AAFC Champions | 1947 |
| Western Conference Champions | 1948 |
| AAFC Champions | 1948 |
| AAFC Champions | 1949 |
| Eastern Conference Champions | 1950 |
| NFL Champions | 1950 |
| Eastern Conference Champions | 1951 |
| Eastern Conference Champions | 1952 |
| Eastern Conference Champions | 1953 |
| Eastern Conference Champions | 1954 |
| NFL Champions | 1954 |
| Eastern Conference Champions | 1955 |
| NFL Champions | 1955 |
| Eastern Conference Champions | 1957 |
| Eastern Conference Champions | 1964 |
| NFL Champions | 1964 |
| Eastern Conference Champions | 1965 |
| Century Division Champions | 1967* |
| Century Division Champions | 1968 |
| Century Division Champions | 1969 |
| AFC Central Champions | 1971 |
| AFC Central Champions | 1980 |
| AFC Central Champions | 1985 |
| AFC Central Champions | 1986 |
| AFC Central Champions | 1987 |
| AFC Central Champions | 1989 |

*From 1967 to 1969, the NFL had four divisions. The Century Division included the Browns, New York Giants, St. Louis Cardinals, and Pittsburgh Steelers.*

**ABOVE:** Paul Brown and owner Art McBride keep kicker Lou Groza well fed.
**BOTTOM**: Sam Rutigliano, the AFC's Coach of the Year in 1979 and 1980.

# Pinpoints

The history of a football team is made up of many smaller stories. These stories take place all over the map—not just in the city a team calls "home." Match the push-pins on these maps to the Team Facts and you will begin to see the story of the Browns unfold!

# TEAM FACTS

**1** Cleveland, Ohio—*The Browns started playing here in 1946.*

**2** New York, New York—*The Browns won the 1947 AAFC championship here.*

**3** Los Angeles, California—*The Browns won the 1950 and 1955 NFL championships here.*

**4** Waukegan, Illinois—*Otto Graham was born here.*

**5** Philadelphia, Pennsylvania—*Leroy Kelly was born here.*

**6** San Diego, California—*Brian Sipe was born here.*

**7** Miami, Florida—*The Browns won their first game here.*

**8** St. Simons Island, Georgia—*Jim Brown was born here.*

**9** Cheyenne, Wyoming—*Don Cockroft was born here.*

**10** Fort Worth, Texas—*Frank Ryan was born here.*

**11** Aiken, South Carolina—*Michael Dean Perry was born here.*

**12** Accra, Ghana—*Ebenezer Ekuban was born here.*

Don Cockroft

# Play Ball

Football is a sport played by two teams on a field that is 100 yards long. The game is divided into four 15-minute quarters. Each team must have 11 players on the field at all times. The group that has the ball is called the offense. The group trying to keep the offense from moving the ball forward is called the defense.

A football game is made up of a series of "plays." Each play starts and ends with a referee's signal. A play begins when the center snaps the ball between his legs to the quarterback. The quarterback then gives the ball to a teammate, throws (or "passes") the ball to a teammate, or runs with the ball himself. The job of the defense is to tackle the player with the ball or stop the quarterback's pass. A play ends when the ball (or player holding the ball) is "down." The offense must move the ball forward at least 10 yards every four downs. If it fails to do so, the other team is given the ball. If the offense has not made 10 yards after three downs—and does not want to risk losing the ball—it can kick (or "punt") the ball to make the other team start from its own end of the field.

At each end of a football field is a goal line, which divides the field from the end zone. A team must run or pass the ball over the goal line to score a touchdown, which counts for six points. After scoring a touchdown, a team can try a short kick for one "extra point," or try again to run or pass across the goal line for two points. Teams can score three points from anywhere on the field by kicking the ball between the goal posts. This is called a field goal.

The defense can score two points if it tackles a player while he is in his own end zone. This is called a safety. The defense can also score points by taking the ball away from the offense and crossing the opposite goal line for a touchdown. The team with the most points after 60 minutes is the winner.

Football may seem like a very hard game to understand, but the more you play and watch football, the more "little things" you are likely to notice. The next time you are at a game, look for these plays:

## PLAY LIST

**BLITZ**—A play where the defense sends extra tacklers after the quarterback. If the quarterback sees a blitz coming, he passes the ball quickly. If he does not, he can end up on the bottom of a very big pile!

**DRAW**—A play where the offense pretends it will pass the ball, and then gives it to a running back. If the offense can "draw" the defense to the quarterback and his receivers, the running back should have lots of room to run.

**FLY PATTERN**—A play where a team's fastest receiver is told to "fly" past the defensive backs for a long pass. Many long touchdowns are scored on this play.

**SQUIB KICK**—A play where the ball is kicked a short distance on purpose. A squib kick is used when the team kicking off does not want the other team's fastest player to catch the ball and run with it.

**SWEEP**—A play where the ball-carrier follows a group of teammates moving sideways to "sweep" the defense out of the way. A good sweep gives the runner a chance to gain a lot of yards before he is tackled or forced out of bounds.

# Glossary

## FOOTBALL WORDS TO KNOW

**AAFC CHAMPIONSHIP**—The game that decided the winner of the All-America Football Conference between 1946 and 1949.

**ALL-AMERICA FOOTBALL CONFERENCE (AAFC)**—A professional league that existed between 1946 and 1949.

**ALL-PRO**—An honor given to the best players at their position at the end of each season. A "first-team" All-Pro is someone who is voted the best of the best.

**AMERICAN FOOTBALL CONFERENCE (AFC)**—One of two groups of teams that make up the National Football League (NFL). The winner of the AFC plays the winner of the National Football Conference (NFC) in the Super Bowl.

**ASSISTANT COACHES**—People that help the head coach run the team. Many assistant coaches specialize in offense or defense. Some are responsible for training players at just one or two positions.

**BLOCKER**—A player who uses his body to protect the ball carrier.

**COLLEGE DRAFT**—The meeting at which NFL teams take turns selecting the best college players each year.

**DEFENSIVE BACKS**—Players who play "back" on defense—usually safeties and cornerbacks.

**DRIVE**—A series of plays that drives the defense back toward its own goal.

**EXPANSION TEAM**—A new team added to a league when it expands.

**FIELD GOAL**—A goal from the field, kicked over the crossbar and between the goal posts. A field goal is worth three points.

**FIVE-MAN LINE**—An arrangement of defensive players that puts five linemen near the ball—usually two defensive ends, two defensive tackles, and a "nose tackle" or "middle guard."

**FREE AGENTS**—Players who do not have a contract with a team, and are free to sign with whichever club they wish.

**MOST VALUABLE PLAYER (MVP)**—The award given each year to the best player; also given to the best player in the Super Bowl.

**NATIONAL FOOTBALL LEAGUE (NFL)**—The league that started in 1920 and still operates today.

**NFL CHAMPIONSHIP**—The game held each year to decide the winner of the league, from 1933 to 1969.

**NORTH DIVISION**—One of the four divisions in each NFL conference. The AFC North was created in 2002.

**PLAYOFFS**—The games played after the season that determine which teams meet for the championship.

**PRESEASON GAME**—A practice game played before the regular season begins. Wins and losses do not count in these games.

**PRO FOOTBALL**—Football played professionally (for money). Professional football players are also called "pros."

**RECEIVERS**—Players whose job is to catch passes.

**ROAD GAMES**—Games played against teams in their stadiums, or "on the road."

**ROOKIE OF THE YEAR**—An award given to the league's best player in his first season.

**RUSHING**—Running with the football. The player who gains the most yards in a season is sometimes called the rushing champion.

**SUPER BOWL**—The championship game of football, played between the winner of the American Football Conference (AFC) and the National Football Conference (NFC).

**TACKLES**—Offensive linemen who play next to the guards. They usually end up blocking the opponent's defensive ends.

**TIGHT END**—An offensive player who lines up next to the tackle. Depending on the play called, he is either a receiver or a blocker.

# OTHER WORDS TO KNOW

**BARRED**—Kept out of or away from.

**CLIMATE**—The normal weather conditions in a place.

**DIAGNOSED**—Found to have an illness or injury.

**FLEXIBLE**—Open-minded and willing to change.

**INCENTIVE**—A good reason to work hard or do something.

**LEUKEMIA**—A type of cancer that affects the bones.

**LOGO**—A company's official picture or symbol.

**LOVE AFFAIR**—An especially close and emotional relationship.

**MAGNIFICENT**—Very grand or beautiful.

**OPTIONS**—Different choices.

**PHYSICS**—A science that studies light, heat sound, electricity, motion and force.

**Ph.D.**—An educational honor that recognizes the highest achievement in a subject.

**PREDICTED**—Said in advance that something would happen.

**RACIAL INCIDENT**—An act of violence or hatred done by someone who does not like people of a different race.

**REPORT**—To present oneself at an assigned time and place.

**TAILBONE**—The bone that protects the base of the spine.

**TRADITIONS**—Beliefs or customs that are handed down from generation to generation.

# Places to Go

## ON THE ROAD

**BROWNS STADIUM**
100 Alfred Lerner Way
Cleveland, OH 44114
(440) 891-5000

**THE PRO FOOTBALL HALL OF FAME**
2121 George Halas Drive NW
Canton, Ohio 44708
(330) 456-8207

## ON THE WEB

**THE NATIONAL FOOTBALL LEAGUE**                    www.nfl.com
  • *Learn more about the National Football League*

**THE CLEVELAND BROWNS**                    www.ClevelandBrowns.com
  • *Learn more about the Cleveland Browns*

**THE PRO FOOTBALL HALL OF FAME**                    www.profootballhof.com
  • *Learn more about football's greatest players*

## ON THE BOOKSHELF

To learn more about the sport of football, look for these books at your library or bookstore:

  • Fleder, Rob–Editor. *The Football Book*. New York, NY.: Sports Illustrated Books, 2005.
  • Kennedy, Mike. *Football*. Danbury, CT.: Franklin Watts, 2003.
  • Savage, Jeff. *Play by Play Football*. Minneapolis, MN.: Lerner Sports, 2004.

47

# Index

PAGE NUMBERS IN **BOLD** REFER TO ILLUSTRATIONS.

## The Team

**MARK STEWART** has written more than 20 books on football, and over 100 sports books for kids. He grew up in New York City during the 1960s rooting for the Giants and Jets, and now takes his two daughters, Mariah and Rachel, to watch them play in their home state of New Jersey. Mark comes from a family of  writers. His grandfather was Sunday Editor of *The New York Times* and his mother was Articles Editor of *The Ladies Home Journal* and *McCall's*. Mark has profiled hundreds of athletes over the last 20 years. He has also written several books about New York and New Jersey. Mark is a graduate of Duke University, with a degree in history. He lives with his daughters and wife, Sarah, overlooking Sandy Hook, NJ.

**JASON AIKENS** is the Collections Curator at the Pro Football Hall of Fame. He is responsible for the preservation of the Pro Football Hall of Fame's collection of artifacts and memorabilia and obtaining new donations of memorabilia from current players and NFL teams. Jason has a Bachelor of Arts in History from Michigan State University and a Masters in History from Western Michigan University where he concentrated on sports history. Jason has been working for the Pro Football Hall of Fame since 1997; before that he was an intern at the College Football Hall of Fame. Jason's family has roots in California  and has been following the St. Louis Rams since their days in Los Angeles, California. He lives with his wife Cynthia and recent addition to the team Angelina in Canton, OH.